CaMPFiRe MaLLORY

For my parents, who sent me to camp.

For my camp friends, who made my days on the shores of
Lake Pokegama some of my best.

For my editor, who gave me the opportunity
to write about it.

And for the real Carine.

Many thanks to you all...
—L. B. F.

For my mom, the true camper
—J. K.

Campfire Mallory

by Laurie Friedman
illustrations by Jennifer Kalis

darbycreek
MINNEAPOLIS

CONTENTS

A WORD FROM MALLORY

My name is Mallory McDonald, like the restaurant, but no relation, and you'll never guess where I'm going!

If you guessed to the bathroom, you guessed wrong.

I'm going to sleep-away camp!

That's right. I'm going to Camp Blue Lake for two weeks, and I'm not the only one who's going. My lifelong best friend, Mary Ann, is going. My big brother, Max, is going. My next door neighbor, Joey, is going, and so is his older sister, Winnie.

And here's the thing about all those people I just mentioned: they're all super excited to go.

Mary Ann says she's excited because she can't wait to meet new people and go on a camp out.

Max says he's excited because he'll get to play lots of baseball.

Joey says he's excited because there's stuff to do that's even more fun than skateboarding, like canoeing and waterskiing.

Even Winnie, who is never excited about anything, says she's excited to go to camp because there won't be any grownups there to boss her around.

Everyone says they can't wait for camp to begin. And the thing is ... they don't have to wait much longer. The bus for Camp Blue Lake leaves Fern Falls in exactly 2 days, 3 hours, 29 minutes, and I'm not sure how many seconds.

But here's what I am sure about: I don't know if I want to be on that bus when it leaves because even though part of me is excited to go to camp, most of me is pretty sure I'd much rather stay at home.

GOOD-BYES

I take papers, pencils, and markers out of my desk and shove them into my backpack. "I can't believe today is our last day!" I say to my desk mate, Pamela.

Pamela takes a stack of folders out of her desk and slides them carefully into her backpack. "It's sad to think we'll never be third-graders again," she says.

Joey walks by our desks carrying a big bag of trash. "How can you even use the word *sad* today? It's our last day of school, we don't have to do any more work, we're about to have a party, and summer vacation starts in two hours."

Even though I'm usually happy about summer vacation, this year things are a little different.

Mrs. Daily taps on Chester, her desk frog. "Class, it's party time!"

"Yeah!" lots of voices shout together.

Mrs. Daily passes around sugar cookies and lemonade. "Who wants to tell the class what you're doing this summer?"

"I do!" shouts a voice near the trash can. "I'm going to sleep-away camp," Joey tells the class. "I'm going to Camp Blue Lake for two weeks, and so is Mallory."

Joey looks in my direction and grins. "There are tons of things to do at camp, like waterskiing and canoeing and tennis. It's going to be so much fun."

Mrs. Daily smiles at Joey like she's having fun just listening to him. "I'm sure you and Mallory are going to have a great time."

Lots of kids tell the class what they're doing over the summer.

Arielle and Danielle are taking dance lessons. Pamela is going to music school. Pete is playing in a basketball league. Hannah is staying at her grandmother's.

I sip my lemonade and think about my own summer plans.

I'm sure there will be things about camp that I like. But the problem is . . . there might also be things I don't like.

I take a tiny bite of my sugar cookie and watch Pamela as she scribbles a note on a scrap of paper. She slides it to my side of the desk. I unfold her note and start reading.

Mallory,
This is our official last note of third grade!
You're going to have so much fun at sleep-
away camp! I wish I could go with you!
I'll miss u!
Hugs!
Pamela

When I finish reading, I refold the note
and slip it into my backpack. I hope
Pamela is right about me having so much
fun at sleep-away camp.

When the bell rings, everyone cheers
and grabs their backpacks. Mrs. Daily hugs
everyone as we walk out of Room 310 for
the last time.

She gives me a tight squeeze. "Mallory,
when you come back to school in the fall, I
want you to stop by my room and tell me

all about summer camp."

"I will," I tell Mrs. Daily. I just hope I have good things to tell her.

When Max and I get home from school, Mom puts a big chocolate cake on the kitchen table. "This is a *congratulations-it's-your-last-day-of-school-and-an-I-can't-believe-you're-leaving-for-camp-in-two-days* cake."

Max grins. "Since it's for two things, can I have two pieces?"

Mom laughs and cuts a thick slice of cake for Max. "Mallory, would you like a big piece too?" Mom asks.

I shake my head. "No thanks. I don't want any cake."

Mom gives me a *since-when-do-you-not-want-cake* look. "Everything OK?"

I shrug my shoulders. "I'm not hungry," I tell Mom. But I don't tell her why I'm not hungry. Just hearing the words *"you're*

leaving for camp in two days" makes me not feel like eating anything, even something as yummy as chocolate cake.

I look at the weekend schedule that Mom posted on the refrigerator.

Friday night: Family dinner (Mmmm!)
Saturday morning: Final packing, Mary Ann and Colleen arrive (Yeah!)
Saturday night: Going-away party at the Winstons' house (Fun!)
Sunday morning: Bus leaves for Camp Blue Lake! (Bye!)

Just thinking about getting on that bus on Sunday morning makes me feel like I ate the whole chocolate cake, and listening to Max doesn't make me feel much better.

"I can't wait to go to camp!" Max says

between bites of cake. "I'm playing baseball every day," he tells Mom.

Mom picks up some cake crumbs Max drops. "That's great," she says. "But don't forget there are a lot of other sports you can try at Camp Blue Lake."

Even though Max loves chocolate cake, he pushes his plate aside. "How could I forget? I'm going to waterski, canoe, play tennis, sail. I'm going to do everything."

Mom smiles at him. "That's the spirit," she says. Then she looks at me. "Mallory, what do you want to try at camp?"

How can I know what I want to try at camp if I don't even know if I want to go to camp? I push my chair back from the table. "I'm going to my room," I tell Mom.

When I get there, I sit down at my desk. I take out a piece of paper and a pencil and start making a list.

10 Reasons why I, Mallory McDonald, Do Not want to go to camp

#1 WHAT IF it rains every day, and I get a head cold?

#2 WHAT IF I get so many mosquito bites, people think I have chicken pox?

#3 WHAT IF I'm allergic to the food and develop a rash?

#4 WHAT IF I fall into the lake and get eaten by a fish or a snake?

#5 WHAT IF there are bats in my bunk?

#6 WHAT IF I don't like the kids in my bunk?

#7 WHAT IF the kids in my bunk don't like me?

#8 WHAT IF my counselor is WEIRD? (I've read about WEIRD counselors!)

#9 WHAT IF Cheeseburger misses me so much she won't eat?

#10 WHAT IF I don't like camp and I want to come home?

WEIRD COUNSELOR

When I finish writing, I lie down on my bed with Cheeseburger and rub her back. She doesn't even know I'm leaving. I wonder how she'll feel while I'm gone.

I lie there for a long time. Then I hear footsteps coming down the hall. Mom and Dad come into my room. Mom sits down on the bed, and Dad pulls up a chair.

"Sweet Potato, are you OK?" asks Dad. "When I came home, Mom said you didn't want any cake and you didn't want to talk about camp."

I hand Dad the list I wrote. "I'm not sure I want to go to camp."

He and Mom look at each other like they were afraid I might say something like that, and they start reading.

When Mom finishes reading, she puts her arm around me. "Mallory, I know you're nervous about going to camp. But I think

you're going to like it once you get there."

Dad brushes my bangs off of my forehead. "You like most things once you give them a chance."

I shrug like I'm not sure I agree. "Going to camp is different. I have to leave you and Mom and Cheeseburger, and I'll be with lots of people I've never met before."

"Don't forget you're going to be there with Mary Ann," says Mom. "The two of you always have fun together no matter what you do."

Dad smiles at me like he's trying to get me to smile back. "A lot of kids have gone to summer camp and had a great time."

"But what if I'm a kid who doesn't?"

"Sweet Potato, give it a chance."

"I'll try," I tell Dad. I hope I'll like camp once I give it a chance. The only question I have is . . . what if I don't?

PANCAKES AND PACKING

"Wake up, Sleepy Head!" Mom pulls back my covers. "Pancakes and packing!"

I pull my covers back over my head. Pancakes sound good, but packing doesn't.

"Rise and shine!" says Mom.

I know there's no sense arguing with Mom. I put on one of the few pairs of shorts that aren't in my camp pile and scoop up Cheeseburger. When we walk into the kitchen, Max is already at the table with a huge plate of pancakes.

"The next time we eat pancakes, it will be around a campfire," he says.

I smile like I can't wait to eat pancakes around a fire, but the truth is, I'm happy eating them around a kitchen table.

"Time to pack," says Mom as soon as we're done. "Mallory, you're first. Then Max." When we get to my room, Mom takes charge. "Shorts and shirts on the bottom. Pajamas on top."

Mom sticks shorts and shirts into my duffel bag. I pick up the pajama pile and run my finger over the *Mallory McDonald* name tape that Mom ironed into the collar of my purple peace sign pajamas. Mary Ann is bringing these pajamas too.

Even though there are lots of things about going to sleep-away camp that I'm not sure I'm going to like, one thing I'm very glad about is that Mary Ann is going with me. I hand Mom the pajama pile, and she puts it into my bag.

I can't believe that in a few hours, Mary Ann and her mom will be in Fern Falls. Now that her mom and Joey's dad are married, we'll be next door neighbors again by this afternoon. And by tomorrow night, we'll be bunk mates too. I bend down and give Cheeseburger a squeeze. "Maybe camp won't be so bad," I whisper to my cat.

Mom takes her head out of my duffel. "Mallory, where's your sunscreen?"

"I don't need it," I tell Mom.

"Of course you do," says Mom. "You don't want your freckles to burn."

I give Mom a *don't-be-such-a-mom* look. She ignores my look and goes into my bathroom to get my sunscreen. When she comes back, she sticks it inside my duffel and puts her arm around me. "I love you, and I want to take care of you."

"I know," I tell Mom. Just thinking about being away at camp and not having Mom around to take care of me makes me feel sad.

Mom hugs me. "You're going to have a wonderful time at camp," she says like she's a mind reader.

"I hope so," I say.

Mom puts my stationery and bath stuff

and rain gear into the duffel and zips it shut. Then she puts her arm around me. "Sweet Potato, if you give camp a chance, I'm sure you'll like it very much."

Mom makes it sound so simple. I hope liking camp is as easy as giving it a chance. I tell my brain not to think about camp for the rest of the morning, but for some reason, camp is the only thing it seems to be thinking about.

When I see Colleen's van pull into the Winstons' driveway next door, I quit thinking about anything except the fact that my best friend is here. "Mom, Mary Ann and Colleen are here!" I shout down the hall. I run next door. When Mary Ann gets out of the van, I give her a huge hug. "Can you believe we're going to be neighbors again?"

Mary Ann hugs me back. "What I can't

24

believe is that we're leaving for sleep-away camp tomorrow morning! I'm so, so, so excited!" she screams.

Frank and Winnie and Joey all come outside while Mary Ann is screaming. The grownups all start hugging. "Are you talking about camp?" Joey asks Mary Ann.

"What else is there to talk about?" she asks. "I can't wait for tomorrow!"

Joey grins. "Me too!"

"Camp is going to be great," says Winnie.

Camp is all anyone talks about all morning and all afternoon too.

After lunch, Mary Ann puts on a camper fashion show. She models the hat, sweatshirt, and flashlight that her mom bought her. Joey shows Mary Ann and me the Whoopee cushion and disappearing ink that his grandpa gave him to take to camp.

Max asks Joey to help him pack his baseball bag. Even Winnie, who almost never talks to anybody, lets Mary Ann and me help her pick out which sunglasses and hair accessories she's taking with her.

At night, camp talk continues. "Which camper wants the first piece of chicken?" Frank asks when we get to his house. He puts a piece on my plate. "Mallory, are the McDonald campers as excited about camp as the Winston campers?" he asks.

I try to decide how to answer that question, but before I say anything, Max answers for me. "I'm super excited!" he says. "Camp is going to be awesome."

"That's great!" says Frank.

I take my chicken and sit down. For once, I hope Max is right. I hope camp will be awesome. I do whatever I do when I want something to happen and I'm not sure it's going to. I pretend like I'm at the wish pond on my street. I close my eyes and make a quick wish. *I wish that camp will be awesome.*

When dinner is over, Mary Ann walks home with me.

"I'm so, so, so glad your mom said I could sleep over," she says.

Even though I love having sleepovers with Mary Ann, I wish Mom had said no since tonight is my last night at home for two whole weeks.

"Let's sleep in our Camp Blue Lake shirts," Mary Ann says.

We put on our matching camp shirts and get into bed. "I don't know how I'll ever fall asleep," says Mary Ann. "I'm so excited."

I tell Mary Ann that I don't know how I'll fall asleep either, but it's not because I'm excited. "I'm a little scared to go to camp,"

I tell Mary Ann.

Mary Ann sits up in bed. "Just think about how much fun we're going to have doing everything together. We'll wear matching clothes and do all the same activities and we'll be bunkmates." Mary Ann grins at me. "We've always had home sleepovers, and now that we're going to be bunkmates, we're going to have camp sleepovers too."

Listening to Mary Ann talk about camp makes it sound like fun. I can picture us wearing matching clothes and doing everything together. And something about camp sleepovers sounds even more fun than home sleepovers.

I smile at Mary Ann. "Maybe camp will be fun," I tell her.

"Of course it will be." Mary Ann turns out the light on my nightstand table. "We

better try to get some sleep. Tomorrow is a big day. Good night, sleep tight, and don't let the bedbugs bite," says Mary Ann.

"Good night, sleep tight, and don't let the bedbugs bite," I say back.

That's what we always say to each other when we go to sleep. I just can't believe the next time we'll be saying it, we'll be sleeping in a bunk bed at Camp Blue Lake.

ON THE BUS

"We're on our way to Camp Blue Lake!" Mary Ann shouts.

She's bouncing up and down in the seat next to me like a beach ball . . . a Camp Blue Lake beach ball. Mary Ann is still wearing the camp shirt she slept in last night, and so am I. In fact, every kid on this bus is wearing a Camp Blue Lake T-shirt.

As the bus rolls away, I wave one last time to Mom, Dad, and Cheeseburger.

Dad waves back and Mom mouths the

word *backpack*. I unzip mine and pull out a
little box wrapped in purple tissue paper. I
unwrap a framed picture of me with
Cheeseburger. Just seeing the picture

makes me feel like I'm going to cry. It was
hard saying good-bye to Mom and Dad.
But it was *really* hard saying good-bye to
Cheeseburger. I felt like crying, but I made
myself hold back my tears. Winnie, Joey,
Max, and Mary Ann didn't look a bit sad to
leave, and I didn't want them to think I was
either.

I look at Mary Ann. I'm so glad she'll be
at camp with me. Just knowing we'll be
doing everything together makes me feel
better. I show her the picture.

"Aw, that's so, so, so cute!" she says.

It is a cute picture. I hold it out in front
of me so I can get a good look.

"That's the cutest cat!" says a voice
behind me. A girl with a huge smile
squeezes into the seat with Mary Ann and
me. She smushes her backpack on the floor
next to ours. "I'm Taylor," she says. "I love

cats! I have one named Tickles."

She reaches into the front pocket of her backpack and pulls out a photo of a fat gray cat. "It was kind of sad to leave him, but I'm used to it," she says.

"How do you get used to leaving your cat?" I ask.

Taylor puts her cat photo back into her backpack. "I left him last year when I went to camp. This is my second summer at Blue Lake. You two must be new."

Mary Ann introduces us like she's our official introducer.

Taylor seems so happy to be on a bus going to sleep-away camp. It's hard for me to imagine someone coming back to camp a second time when I'm not even sure I'm going to like going once. "Is camp fun?" I ask Taylor.

"Camp is fantastic!" she says. "There's

so much fun stuff to do."

"Like what?" I ask. I want to know what Taylor thinks is fun. Maybe if I like some of the same things she likes, I'll like camp as much as she does.

"My favorite things are photography, archery, outdoor cooking, swimming, waterskiing, pottery making, going on the overnight, and Color War," says Taylor.

It sounds like Taylor likes just about everything. Some of the things she said sound fun to me too, like pottery making. Maybe I'll make a bowl for Cheeseburger.

"When you say *overnight,* you mean sleeping in tents and making s'mores over a fire?" asks Mary Ann.

Taylor grins. "That's what I mean."

Mary Ann high-fives Taylor. "I can't wait to go on the overnight."

Winnie leans across the aisle. "Did someone say we have to sleep in tents?" She makes an *I'm-not-a-sleeping-in-tents-kind-of-girl* face.

Taylor laughs. "It's fun, I promise."

I think about what Mom and Dad said about giving it a chance. Maybe it won't be so hard to do.

Taylor takes a pack of bubble gum out of her backpack and gives Mary Ann and me a piece. She pops two pieces into her own mouth. "So how old are you?"

Mary Ann answers for us. "We're nine and going into fourth grade."

"Me too!" says Taylor. Then she blows a bubble. Mary Ann and I watch as it gets bigger and bigger. When it gets really big, Taylor takes it out of her mouth and puts it on her finger. She holds it up high so everyone sitting around us can see it.

Joey whistles when he sees it.

"Wow! Wow! Wow!" says Mary Ann.

Taylor laughs. "I've never heard anyone say things three times."

Mary Ann puts her arm around me.

"Mallory and I always do."

All of a sudden, Taylor looks a little shy. "Maybe I can do it too?"

Mary Ann puts her other arm around Taylor. "Why not? We can all do it," she says, looking at me like she's sure I'll approve of the idea.

"Sure," I nod. I can picture the three of us at camp doing lots of things together.

A group of boys in the seat behind us shoot paper balls over our heads. One lands in my hair and Taylor picks it out for me. "Ignore them," she says.

"Thanks," I say when Taylor is done getting the paper out of my hair. With friends like Mary Ann and Taylor, camp might actually be fun.

"Campers, get ready! We're almost at camp," shouts a counselor from the front of the bus. She has long blond hair pulled

up in a ponytail on top of her head.

"That's Jolie," explains Taylor. "She's the camp song leader."

"She's so pretty," says Mary Ann.

"And so sweet," says Taylor. "I'd love to have her as my counselor."

"That would be fun, fun, fun," I say.

Mary Ann and Taylor laugh.

"OK, campers, who's ready to make some noise?" Jolie shouts.

Everyone starts screaming and cheering as the bus turns off the main road onto a dirt road. It pulls to a stop in front of a long brown building. A *Welcome Blue Lake Campers!* sign hangs from the roof. There's more cheering as everyone grabs backpacks, tennis rackets, and pillows. Joey and Max are the first ones off the bus. Winnie is right behind them.

"C'mon!" shouts Taylor. "It's time for the

fun to begin!"

Mary Ann and I grab our backpacks and follow Taylor off the bus. I take my first look around what I'm going to call home for the next two weeks. Then I cross my toes.

I sure hope Taylor was right when she said it's time for the fun to begin.

CAMP BLUE LAKE

**Camp Blue Lake Words of Wisdom:
Get dirty and stay dirty.**

"Who wants bug juice?" A guy with an apron walks around with a tray of paper cups filled with purple liquid. I look inside the cups. All I see is Kool-Aid. No bugs.

But I'm still not sure I want to drink something called bug juice.

"BUG JUICE!" screams a group of boys. They all grab cups off the tray. Joey and Max grab some too. When they do, bug juice splashes all over them . . . and me!

None of the boys seem to care. But I do. My T-shirt looks like it should say Camp Purple Spot, not Camp Blue Lake.

"Welcome to camp, everyone!" a tall, skinny man standing on a platform shouts through a megaphone.

"That's Uncle Al," Taylor explains to Mary Ann and me.

"He's the camp director."

"Who's ready to have fun?" he asks.

"Bring it on!" a group of teenagery-looking kids behind me shouts.

"They're the oldest campers," Taylor tells us. "Some of them have been here for seven years. It's their last year. They're totally into camp."

I look at them. They all have their arms around each other. They look like they're

into camp. I try to picture myself like them one day. But it's hard to do.

Taylor shifts her backpack from one shoulder to the other. "I bet Uncle Al makes the same *welcome-to-camp* speech he made last summer."

"Welcome back returning campers! It's great to see all of you. We have a lot of new faces today. I expect all you old-timers to help out the newbies."

I never thought of myself as a *newbie,* but I guess that's what I am.

"New campers, welcome to Camp Blue Lake!" says Uncle Al. "We hope you love every minute of your home away from home."

"Sounds just like last year," Taylor says with a grin.

Even though Taylor's heard what he has to say before, she looks like she's happy to hear it again. I feel like Taylor's T-shirt should say *Miss Camp Blue Lake*. She knows everything about camp. I can see how having an *oldie* around could come in handy.

"New campers, we don't want anyone getting lost, so let me tell you a little bit about the camp." He points up a hill to the building behind him. "That's the Lodge. We eat all of our meals in there."

"Those are meals?" a boy in the group behind me shouts out.

The whole group starts laughing. Taylor laughs too. "Camp Blue Lake isn't exactly known for its food."

Uncle Al pretends like his feelings are hurt, but I can tell they're really not. "None of that," he says. He points in the opposite direction. "Down the hill are the Canteen, the Nature Shed, the Craft Shop, and beautiful Blue Lake."

I turn in the direction he's pointing.
What I see looks more brown than blue.
Mary Ann holds her nose. "Does the lake
smell as bad as it looks?"

Taylor laughs. "You're so funny!" she
says to Mary Ann.

"Where's the baseball field?" Max yells
out.

Uncle Al points up the hill.

"Girls, bunks are that direction," Uncle Al

says pointing down a dirt path to his left. Then he motions with his megaphone to the right. "Boys' bunks are that direction."

"Boys' and girls' bunks are on opposite sides of the lake?" Winnie asks.

Taylor nods. Winnie looks more disappointed than she did when she found out she was going to have to sleep in a tent.

"When do we get to go to our bunks?" Joey asks from behind me.

Taylor starts to answer, but before she gets to, Uncle Al waves his megaphone in the air. "I know everybody is excited to get to their cabins, but first, it's time for the Camp Blue Lake Words of Wisdom."

Everyone behind me groans.

"No groaning, just a drum roll," says Uncle Al with a big smile.

The sound of kids slapping their knees

fills the air.

"Uncle Al loves to give speeches about the *meaning of camp,*" Taylor tells us.

"The Camp Blue Lake Words of Wisdom for the day are . . . *Get dirty and stay dirty.*" Some kids cheer when Uncle Al says that, like they love the idea of getting dirty and staying dirty. I look down at my spotty T-shirt. I'm not sure I have a choice.

"Now, the moment you've all been waiting for," says Uncle Al. "Time for bunk assignments."

"Assignments? Are we at camp or school?" Joey asks.

The word *assignments* doesn't sound like something I thought I'd hear at camp. "What are bunk assignments?" I ask Taylor.

Taylor blows a big bubble. After it pops, she starts talking. "Bunk assignments are when the counselors tell you what bunk you're in and who's in it with you."

Taylor loops one arm through mine and the other through Mary Ann's. "There are two nine-year-old-girl bunks. The Lucky Ducks and the Kool Kats. So chances are pretty good that we'll all be together."

Even though Taylor said the chances are *pretty good*, I feel *pretty bad*. I didn't know there were two nine-year-old bunks. What if Mary Ann and I aren't together? I cross my toes that that *won't* happen.

"OK," says Uncle Al. "I'm going to call out your age groups and tell you where to meet your bunk counselors. They will give you your bunk assignments."

Uncle Al points the seven- and eight-year-olds toward their counselors. "Nine-year-old girls under the spruce tree, and nine-year-old boys by the tire swing," he says.

"This way," says Taylor. She motions for Mary Ann and me to follow her.

"See you later," says Joey as he heads toward the tire swing.

Mary Ann and I follow Taylor. When we get there, two counselors are waiting. Jolie, from the bus, is there with her guitar. The other counselor has on a bathing suit and a whistle around her neck.

"Hi girls, I'm Jolie." She plays a chord on her guitar. "I'm the counselor of the Kool Kats," she says in a sing-song voice.

The other counselor blows her whistle. I jump, and so do a lot of other girls. "I'm Sandy. I'm the waterfront director and the counselor of the Lucky Ducks."

"I hope we're all Kool Kats," whispers Taylor.

I look at Mary Ann and cross my toes extra hard. It would be fun to all be Kool

Kats, but what I really hope is that whatever I am, Mary Ann is one too.

Everyone is quiet while we wait for Jolie and Sandy to read the bunk assignments. Jolie goes first. She strums her guitar and smiles. Then she reads names off of a list.

I hear a *Chelsea,* a *Mia,* a *Jordan,* a *Lee,* a *Mary Ann,* and a *Taylor.* I wait to hear a *Mallory* too, but that's not what I hear.

Jolie plays a long, happy chord on her guitar. "If I read your name, follow me!"

Sandy blows her whistle again. "If you didn't hear your name, that means you're a Lucky Duck, and you're with me."

Campers start falling in line behind their counselors. Even though it's really hot outside, my feet feel like they're frozen to the ground. I can't believe I'm in one bunk, and Mary Ann is in another.

"We're together!" I hear Taylor say to

Mary Ann as they start to follow Jolie.

I turn around and see Taylor jumping up and down like she's super excited that she and Mary Ann are in the same bunk. Mary Ann gives me an *it-stinks-we're-not-in-the-same-bunk* look. But I can tell she thinks it's cool that she's a Kat.

Of all the things that I thought might go wrong at camp, this wasn't one of them. In my head, I had pictured Mary Ann and me doing everything together. Now Mary Ann is going to be doing everything together with somebody else.

Sandy blows her whistle again. "Lucky Ducks, follow me."

I get in line and follow Sandy and five other girls down the hill.

I know I'm a Lucky Duck, but right now, I sure don't feel like one.

THE LUCKY DUCKS

Camp Blue Lake Words of Wisdom:
Don't count the days,
make the days count.

"Duckies, we're this way!" says Sandy.
All six Lucky Ducks follow Sandy toward
a row of brown bunks.

A girl with a long, thick ponytail on the side of her head falls in line beside me. When she walks, her hair bounces around like a horse's tail and hits me in the face.

"Sorry about that," says the girl. She grabs her ponytail like she's trying to stop it from misbehaving, but when she does, she drops her tennis racket, pillow, and two board games.

I bend down to pick them up. I start to hand them to her, but she's carrying a backpack, hiking boots, a stuffed bear, scuba gear, and a sleeping bag. I tuck her pillow under one arm and her tennis racket and board games under the other.

"Thanks! That's better!" she says.

Maybe better for her, but I feel like a moving truck.

"I'm Carine Green," says the girl. "My names rhyme. Carine and Green. So what's your name?"

"Mallory McDonald, like the restaurant but no relation."

Carine smiles like she's glad she met me. "Hi, Mallory McDonald."

I smile like I'm glad I met her too. But I can't help thinking that if I'd been in the same bunk as Mary Ann and Taylor, I wouldn't have met her and I definitely wouldn't be carrying her pillow and her tennis racket and her board games.

"I brought a lot," she says like she can tell what I'm thinking. "My mom says I take too much stuff wherever I go, but that's me. I'm a *stuff* lover. I'm also a green lover. If you ask me, you can never have too much green."

I look down at the green pillow and bear I'm carrying. Carine's not kidding about liking green. "My favorite color is purple," I tell her. When I say that, I can't help thinking about Mary Ann. We have the same favorite color.

I see Mary Ann and Taylor and the rest of the Kool Kats walking ahead of us. Mary Ann has her arm through Taylor's. I watch as they stop in front of a little wooden cabin and walk inside. I swallow hard. I wish I was walking inside with them.

We walk past another wooden cabin and Sandy blows her whistle. "Duckies, we're home," she says. Carine, four other girls, and I all follow Sandy inside.

I put Carine's stuff down, then I look
around. There are three sets of empty
shelves and bunk beds, and a single bed
that's already made up. There's a sign in
the shape of an inner tube over the made-
up bed that says: *Sandy sleeps here.*

Sandy blows her whistle. "Duckies, make a circle. Time to meet your cabin mates."

Carine pats an empty spot on the floor next to her. "Mallory, sit here."

I can't believe I'm sitting in a circle with a bunch of people I've never met before today and I'm going to be living with them for the next two weeks. I look at Carine. I wish I could wiggle my nose and turn her into Mary Ann. But I know that won't work.

I pretend like I'm at the wish pond and make a different wish. *I wish I will like these people I'm living with for the next two weeks.*

"OK, everyone," Sandy says after we're all seated. "I'd like everyone to introduce themselves. I'll start and we'll go around the circle. I'm Sandy, and I love swimming." Sandy blows her whistle and points to a girl with curly red hair.

"I'm Nikki," says the girl. "This is my

second summer at camp. I like to swim and play tennis." She grins and looks at me. "And I like your hair."

Nikki and I have the exact same color hair. I grin back at her.

Sandy blows her whistle again. "Your turn," she says to the next girl.

A girl with big blue eyes starts talking. "I'm Natalie. This is my second summer at Blue Lake. I love photography and arts and crafts." Natalie sticks her hands out so everyone can see them. Her fingernails match her eyes. "I also love painting nails, so if anyone needs a manicure or a pedicure, just come see me."

I bet Natalie picked blue for the same reason I picked it. We're at Camp *Blue* Lake. I wiggle my light blue fingers in front of Natalie, and she smiles.

The next girl to introduce herself is

Brooke. It's her first summer at camp, and she loves comic books. She pulls a stack of them out of her backpack. "I brought lots if anyone wants to borrow them."

I've never seen so many comic books. I smile at Brooke. I can't wait to read some of her comic books.

Sandy blows the whistle again, and this time Molly introduces herself. "This is my first summer at Blue Lake, and I'm excited about camp, but I'm also a little sad because I had to leave my dog at home." She pulls a framed picture of a fluffy white dog out of her backpack. "This is Lucy."

I get my picture of Cheeseburger out to show Molly. Everyone wants to see the pet pictures, so we pass them around the circle.

When we're done, Sandy calls on Carine.

"I'm Carine Green. I'm not a pet person. But I'm a stuff person. I brought so much stuff with me on the bus to camp that Mallory had to help me carry it to the bunk. Thanks again, Mallory." She smiles at me like she really appreciated my help.

"It was no big deal," I tell Carine. I didn't mind carrying her stuff, but for some reason, I do mind her thanking me in front of everyone.

I think about what Mom and Dad said about giving things a chance. It's going to be easy to give most of the girls in my bunk a chance, but I don't know how easy it's going to be to give Carine a chance. I don't know her well yet, and even though she seems nice, there's something about her that's kind of annoying.

Sandy blows her whistle and points to me.

"I'm Mallory McDonald, like the restaurant, but no relation. This is my first summer at camp, and I hope it's going to be fun."

"OK," says Sandy when I'm done introducing myself. "The next thing we have to do is pick bunkmates. Choose carefully. You and your bunkmate not only share a bed and shelves, but you'll be partners in lots of other ways too."

I think about Mary Ann. We were supposed to be bunkmates. I look around my bunk. Even though I wanted Mary Ann to be my bunkmate, some of the girls in my bunk seem nice.

I think I'd like being bunkmates with Natalie or Molly, or even Nikki or Brooke. But before I have a chance to choose one of them, someone chooses me.

"I call Mallory!" screams Carine. She grabs my hand like I'm hers. Before I have a chance to say anything, Nikki picks

Natalie, and Brooke and Molly pair up.

"OK," says Sandy. "Time to unpack and get settled in. But first I want to read you some words of wisdom from Uncle Al."

The old campers make a drum roll on their knees and the new campers follow along. *"Don't count the days, make the days count,"* says Sandy.

When she finishes reading, Carine grabs my hand. "C'mon, let's unpack. I'll help you, and then you can help me, which might take forever because I have tons of stuff." As Carine pulls me towards our shelves, her ponytail hits me in the face again.

I think about Uncle Al's Words of Wisdom. I can't help thinking that I have one day down and thirteen to go as Carine Green's bunkmate.

LETTERS

"Last one to the mail shack is a rotten egg!" Joey says as we leave the Lodge.

I race him to the place we go every day after lunch to see who got mail.

Even though Joey is usually faster, today, I get there first. I've been at camp three whole days, and I haven't gotten a letter yet. I cross my toes that today will be my lucky day.

"Anything for Mallory McDonald?" I ask Liz, the mail counselor. She looks in her

stack and hands me a light purple envelope. "From Cheeseburger McDonald," she says with a smile as she reads from the return address.

Winnie rolls her eyes when she hears who the letter is from. But I ignore her. I take my envelope and go sit on a nearby stump. I can't wait to read my letter.

Dear Mallory,

Hi! Hi! Hi! How's camp? Are you having a great time? I can't wait to hear EVERYTHING! Even though I miss you a lot, I hope you're having tons of fun and doing lots of cool stuff and making loads of new friends. (Just no new cat friends!)

You aren't missing a thing at home. I promise! Everything is exactly the same as when you left. Actually, one thing is different. I learned how to write (Mom taught me) so I can write a letter to you. When you have a chance, write back and tell me how you're doing and what you're doing. I want to hear EVERYTHING! (So do Mom and Dad!)

Lots of love,
Your cat, Cheeseburger

P.S. Tell Mary Ann hi! And Max too! (Mom made me add in the Max part!)

When I finish reading, I refold my letter and stick it back into the envelope. I see Mary Ann and Taylor heading back to their cabin for rest hour. I run to catch up with them. "Look what I got!" I show Mary Ann my letter from Cheeseburger.

She takes it from me and starts reading. "Oh, that's so, so, so cute!" She shows Taylor that the letter is from my cat.

"Oh, that is so, so, so cute!" says Taylor.

They both laugh at the same time, like it's fun to say things three times together. But I don't laugh. Even though I said it was OK for Taylor to say things three times, I didn't think Taylor and Mary Ann would be saying things together, without me.

"So what activity does your bunk have after rest hour?" Mary Ann asks.

I try to picture the Lucky Duck Activity Schedule that Sandy tacked on the wall of our cabin. "I think we have archery and photography."

"The Kool Kats have swimming and canoeing," says Taylor. Then she sticks her arm through Mary Ann's. "C'mon! We have to hurry back to our bunk to change into our bathing suits and write letters."

Mary Ann and Taylor wave.

I wish I was running off with them to change into my bathing suit and write letters. I refold my letter and walk into my own bunk. When I get there, everyone is already on their beds writing letters.

"Mallory, where have you been?" asks Carine. "You're supposed to be on your bed writing letters because it's letter writing day." Carine pats her bed. "You can sit on my bed with me and write letters if you want to."

"Thanks, but I'll just sit on my own bed,"

I tell Carine.

I take my clipboard from my shelves. I really don't want to write my letter on Carine's bed. Even though it's nice of her to offer, there are things I want to write in my letter that I don't want Carine to see. I climb up to my bed and take a sheet of purple paper out of my clipboard. Then I take a deep breath.

"Mallory, everything OK?" asks Sandy.

I nod like everything is OK. But I know if I tried to explain to Sandy that a lot of the things Carine does are really starting to bug me, she would just say something about giving people a chance.

I take a purple gel pen out of my clipboard and start writing to someone I know will understand.

Day 3, Camp Blue Lake

Dear Cheeseburger,
I am so proud of you for being able to write. I don't know if Mom has taught you to read, but if not, get her to read this letter to you and tell her it's a V.I.L. (That's short for a Very Important Letter.)
Do you know the expression so far so

good? Well, I'm changing it to *so far NOT so good,* because I got to camp three days ago, and even though some good things have happened to me since I got here (like getting doughnuts for break-fast and the Fastest Paddler Award in canoeing), a lot of *not so good* things have happened to me too.

The first not so good thing is that Mary Ann and I are in different bunks. Mary Ann is a Kool Kat and I'm a Lucky Duck.

But here's what's not lucky about that: I have a V.A.B. (that's short for Very Annoying Bunkmate) named Carine. If you're wondering what makes Carine annoying, I'll tell you. She brought WAY too much stuff to camp, and it's a BIG problem!!!

Yesterday when Nurse Shelby (she's

the nurse and the cabin inspector) came for cabin checks, our cabin got a STINKO (which means our bunk was a big mess). Nurse Shelby said that all of the other girls bunks got WHOOPIES (which means their bunks were super neat) and that the reason our bunk got a STINKO was because Carine's shelves (which happen to be mine too because we share) were a big mess.

Then she said that Carine and I had to skip the after-dinner marshmallow roast and sing-a-long and stay in the bunk to clean up our shelves. (You know how much I hate folding and how much I love marshmallows!)

But guess what? Because of Carine, roasted marshmallows weren't the only thing I had to miss. I had to miss water-skiing too.

Here's what happened.

Yesterday, when it was time for our bunk to go waterskiing, Carine couldn't find her flip-flops and sun hat. My counselor made me stay and help her.

By the time we found her flip-flops and sun hat, and the ski dock (which is hard to find, see illustration below), it was time for our bunk to go to Arts and

Crafts, so Carine and I never got to ski.

Please tell Mom and Dad that I know they would say to give Carine a chance, but I don't have time to do that right now because rest hour will be over soon and my bunk has archery and photography this afternoon.

OK. G.2.G.S.B.A.A. (That's short for Got To Go Shoot Bows And Arrows.)

Big huge hugs and kisses (and a few tears at night because I'm sharing a bed with Carine and not you or Mary Ann),

Mallory

P.S. When I cried, I had to wipe my nose on my laundry bag (which is hanging off the side of my bed) because I didn't have a tissue.

P.P.S. Your picture is right next to my pillow, and I'm making you a new bowl in Arts and Crafts.

P.P.P.S. Tell Mom and Dad that Max said if I write to say *hi*. I told him he should write his own letter, but he said that parents know it's a good sign if their kids don't write because it means they are having so much fun at camp that they don't have time to write. Do you think that's true?

P.P.P.P.S. Guess what? There are bats in my cabin! You heard right. And guess what else? I sleep in the top bunk so it is very easy for them to get me when they

come out at night. I am an official C.L.B.H.
(That is short for Cat Lover, Bat Hater.)

P.P.P.P.P.S. There's one thing I love about
camp, and it's called Cilk and Mookies. It's
really Milk and Cookies, but that is the
cute name Uncle Al made up for what he
calls a Camp Blue Lake tradition. When I
get home, I'm going to make it a Wish
Pond Road tradition. You can have the
Cilk and I'll eat the Mookies. Doesn't that
sound like fun?

P.P.P.P.P.P. (I know that's a lot of P's) S.
Keep your paws crossed that tomorrow
will be fun. It's Waterfront Day at Camp
Blue Lake, and everyone in my bunk who
was here last year says it is one of the
best days at camp!!!

BUDDY CHECK

**Camp Blue Lake Words of Wisdom:
Everyone deserves a second chance.**

Sandy blows her whistle. "Attention campers!" she yells.

A beach full of campers turns towards the lifeguard stand.

"Welcome to Waterfront Day!" Sandy says through a giant megaphone. "We've got lots of fun activities planned, but we have a few safety rules that everyone needs to follow." She reads from a clipboard. "Safety rule #1: No horse play."

"I didn't know there were horses on the beach," says Max from behind me. A group of his friends start laughing.

The name of their bunk is the Terrifying Tigers, but they should be called the Laughing Hyenas because that's what they sound like.

Sandy blows her whistle at them, and they stop laughing. She keeps reading.

"Safety rule #2: No running on the dock. And safety rule #3: Stick with your buddy."

Sandy gets a very serious *waterfront-director* look on her face. "If you don't, there'll be consequences. Newbies, just ask any old-timer what I'm talking about."

When Sandy says that, the boys behind me groan, and so do the old campers in my bunk. "Buddy checks are the worst," says Natalie.

I look at Natalie over the top of my sunglasses. "What's a buddy check?"

Nikki answers for her. "When Sandy blows her whistle and yells *Buddy Check,* you have to find your buddy, hold hands, and raise your arms in the air. They do it to make sure no one is missing."

I stick my toe in the sandy beach and dig a little hole with it.

"Are there really consequences?" I ask.

Natalie laughs and points to the boat shed. "If you don't raise hands with your buddy at *Buddy Check*, you and your buddy have to wear one of those ugly old life jackets for the rest of the day."

I look over at the boat shed. There's a whole row of faded orange life jackets hanging on the side of it. "Yuck!" I say.

"Totally yuck," says Nikki. "Someone always ends up wearing them because they can't find their buddy."

I look at Carine, who's my bunkmate and my buddy. I definitely don't want to wear one of those orange life jackets around all day. "Let's stick together," I say.

Carine loops her arm through mine. "We'll stick together like glue."

I look at the life jackets, and then I look at Carine. Even though I'm not sure I want to be stuck together all day, it's better than wearing one of those old life jackets.

"OK, everyone," says Sandy. "Uncle Al has a list of stations and activities. Find out from him where your bunk is supposed to be, and HAVE FUN!"

Everyone cheers. Winnie's bunk starts setting up towels and beach blankets. The younger kids splash into the water with their counselors. The Lucky Ducks head over to Uncle Al to see where we're supposed to go first.

"The Lucky Ducks and the Kool Kats are competing in the water relay." Uncle Al points us to the end of the dock.

Even though we're competing against each other, I'm glad our bunk is doing something with the Kool Kats. Ever since I got to camp, I feel like I've barely seen Mary Ann. I run to catch up with Mary Ann and Taylor, who are halfway down the dock.

When I do, Sandy blows her whistle. "Mallory, no running on the dock!"

"Mallory, wait up," Carine calls after me.

I slow down. I want to see my best friend, but I don't want to lose my buddy.

When all of the Lucky Ducks and the Kool Kats get to the end of the dock, I stick my arm through Mary Ann's. "So how do you like camp so far?" I ask.

"It's great, great, great!" says Mary Ann. "How about you?"

"I like parts of it," I tell her. But before I

can tell her about the parts I don't like, Carine grabs me. "C'mon Mallory! The relay is about to start." She pulls me over to where the rest of my bunk is standing on the dock.

Annie, the swim counselor, tells us all to get ready.

I watch as Taylor, Mary Ann, and the rest of the Kool Kats huddle together. "Go Kool Kats!" they scream.

The Lucky Ducks huddle too. "Let's go Lucky Ducks!" we all scream.

Even though I want to win the relay, part of me can't help wishing I was screaming the same thing as Mary Ann.

"Yeah!" my bunk screams as we take turns jumping into the water and swimming across the roped-off area and back.

Our screaming works. We beat the Kool Kats at the water relay.

"All nine-year-old boys and girls to the diving dock for the Crazy Dive," Uncle Al announces when the water relay is over.

"That was so much fun!" Carine says as we walk to the diving dock.

"Boo hoo!" I hear Taylor say to Mary Ann. "I can't believe the Lucky Ducks beat us. We're going to win the Crazy Dive," she says like she's a cheerleader.

As I walk to the diving dock, I feel like I just swallowed a big mouthful of lake water. Not only are Mary Ann and I in different bunks, now we're competing against each other. This was not at all what I pictured camp to be like.

All of the nine-year-old girls and boys, including Joey's bunk, meet on the diving platform. "Craziest dive wins the day!"

announces Mike, the diving counselor.

I watch as kids start flipping and flopping off of the dock.

"Hey Mallory, watch this!" Joey laughs as he and the boys from his bunk belly flop into the lake.

When it's the Lucky Ducks' turn, we quack and flap our arms like real ducks.

When the Kool Kats go, they all purr and crawl down the dock on all fours like they're real cats.

"The Kool Kats win the Crazy Dive!" Mike says after everyone has had a turn.

The Kool Kats all hug each other. "We win! We win! We win!" Taylor screams.

"Free Swim!" Sandy announces from the lifeguard stand.

"Free Swim is fun swim," Natalie says as we all jump into the lake.

I agree with Natalie. Free Swim will be

fun. The Lucky Ducks and Kool Kats swim together to the middle of the swim area. I can finally spend time with Mary Ann. I paddle over to where Mary Ann and Taylor are floating on their backs.

"Do you guys want to have a contest to see who can float on their backs the longest?" I ask Taylor and Mary Ann.

"Sure!" they say at the same time.

We all start floating. "I think I'm getting seasick," I say.

"I think I'm getting lake sick!" says Mary Ann.

We all start laughing and stop floating.

"Let's have a handstand contest," says Taylor.

I start to dive under water, when I hear a whistle. "Buddy check!" Sandy announces through her megaphone.

Everyone around me starts scrambling

around to find their buddy. Sets of hands go up in the air. I look for Carine. She was right next to me when we started Free Swim, but now I don't see her.

Sandy blows her whistle again. "Find your buddy."

I look on the dock and on the beach. I still don't see my buddy. "Carine!" I shout her name so she can hear me. Sets of hands continue going up all around me.

Sandy blows her whistle one more time. "Last call for Buddy Check."

Sets of camper hands are up all over the waterfront. There's only one hand that's not holding someone else's, and that hand is mine.

"Mallory, where's Carine?" Sandy calls out from the lifeguard stand.

Even though the water is cold, I feel hot inside. "I don't know where she is."

Sandy blows her whistle three times and counselors everywhere spring into action looking for Carine and shouting her name. I call out her name too.

She's supposed to be here for Buddy Check and now everyone, including me, is trying to find her.

"I've got her!" A counselor is walking down the hill towards the beach holding Carine's arm. I run over to the lifeguard stand.

Sandy climbs down from her post. Her face is as white as her megaphone. "Carine, where were you?" she asks.

"I had to go to the bathroom," says Carine.

Sandy looks upset. "Carine, you're supposed to stay with your buddy." Sandy looks at me like she's upset with me too. "Mallory, you should have gone with her."

"I didn't even know Carine was going to the bathroom," I tell Sandy.

But Sandy shakes her head like that's not a good excuse. "You girls are going to have to learn to work together," says Sandy. She walks over to the boat shed and takes two life jackets off of their

hooks. She slips them over our heads. "You both have to wear these through dinner."

I hear giggling around us as Sandy straps the jackets around us.

"I can't believe someone in our bunk has to wear these," says Nikki.

Natalie makes a *this-is-so-embarrassing-for-our-whole-bunk* face.

Max walks by and shakes his head. "Do me a favor and don't tell anyone we know each other," he mumbles.

Carine looks at me. "Sorry, Mallory, I should have told you I was leaving."

I nod my head like it's OK, but it's really not. Waterfront Day was supposed to be one of the best days at Camp Blue Lake, and it turned out to be the worst.

All Carine had to do was tell me she had to go to the bathroom and we wouldn't be wearing these stupid life jackets and no one would be laughing at us. I think about Uncle Al's Words of Wisdom this morning. At breakfast, he said that everyone deserves a second chance.

I feel like I've given Carine Green lots of chances. But I'm starting to wonder how many chances one girl needs.

A BAD DAY

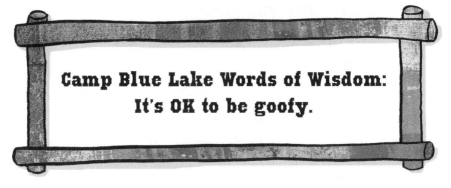

**Camp Blue Lake Words of Wisdom:
It's OK to be goofy.**

I roll over in my bed. I hear the sound of
a bell in the background. At first, I think
it's a dream, but then I hear a loud whistle.
"Rise and shine, Duckies!" says Sandy.

I pull my covers back over my head. This

morning I want to sleep as long as I can.
But someone pulls my covers off of me.
"Mallory, time to get up!" says Carine.

Sandy blows her whistle again. "Up and
at 'em, Duckies. We've got a big day!"
Sandy reads from the daily schedule as
everyone in my bunk gets dressed.
"Outdoor cooking this morning, and drama
and canoeing after lunch."

"Outdoor cooking is so much fun,"
Natalie says.

Nikki nods like she agrees. "Nature Bob
teaches us how to cook over a campfire so
we'll know what to do when we go on the
overnight."

"Is the overnight fun?" Molly asks.

Nikki and Natalie high-five each other.
"It's the best," says Natalie.

Nikki shakes her head like she agrees.
"All the girls go one night and the boys go

another. We sleep in tents and cook our food over a campfire. You'll love it."

Sandy smiles. "It's nice to see everyone so happy this morning," she says.

Everyone is happy, including me. It sounds like fun to cook things over a fire. I pop out of bed and throw on shorts and a shirt. I slide my feet into my flip-flops.

When I get to the Lodge, everyone is talking about the overnight.

"Mallory are you psyched to go on the overnight?" Joey asks me.

"Too bad it's only for one night," Max says to me.

"I can't believe we have to sleep in tents!" says Winnie.

"The overnight is going to be fun, fun, fun!" says Taylor.

I take some pancakes and a yogurt from the breakfast buffet and sit down at the

table with my bunk. I think the overnight is going to be fun too.

When breakfast is over, Uncle Al tells everyone that it's time to go to our morning activities. "But first, some words of wisdom," he says with a grin. "The Camp Blue Lake Words of Wisdom for today are . . . *It's OK to be goofy.*"

There's lots of groaning and some eye rolling too.

"Now can we go?" Molly asks Sandy.

Sandy smiles. "Now we can go."

My bunk and the Kool Kats meet at the Nature Shed.

"Welcome to the wonderful world of nature," says a counselor with a long beard. "I'm Nature Bob, and I'm going to help you girls get prepared for the overnight."

Mary Ann jumps up and down. "Taylor

says we're going to have so, so, so much fun on the overnight. She says it's the best night of camp. I can't wait to go!"

"Neither can I. Maybe we'll get to sleep in the same tent," I say.

"We can wear our matching campfire pajamas," says Mary Ann.

Now it's my turn to jump up and down. The overnight sounds like so much fun.

Nature Bob shows us how to pitch tents and make a campfire. "Today, we're going to learn how to make french fries. Everything tastes better when you cook it over a fire," he says.

"I agree," says Natalie. "Last year, we made french fries and they were even better than the ones from McDonald's."

"I love McDonald's fries. If these are better, I can't wait to try them," I say.

Nature Bob puts a big pot filled with oil

on the fire. Then he takes out a box full of knives.

"Everyone, please pair up with your bunkmates." He walks around and gives each pair of bunkmates a knife and a potato.

"I'm giving each of you a knife to cut your potato into slices. Please be careful because the knives are sharp. When you're done slicing, we'll cook the potatoes in the oil." He smiles. "And then we'll have the world's tastiest french fries."

"I can't wait to taste the world's tastiest french fries," I tell Carine as Nature Bob gives us our knife.

Carine giggles. "Neither can I."

"OK," says Nature Bob when he's done passing out the knives. "Start slicing."

All around us, pairs of bunkmates start slicing potatoes.

Carine and I both look at our knife. "You first," says Carine.

The knife looks sharp. Part of me can't wait to try the world's tastiest french fries,

but part of me doesn't want to cut that potato with that knife. "You go ahead," I say.

But Carine doesn't move. "I don't like using sharp knives," she says softly.

The truth is . . . neither do I. "We have to cut the potato," I whisper to Carine. "What are we going to do?"

Carine scratches her head like she's trying to think of something.

"I've got it!" she says, like a light bulb just lit up in her brain. "Let's tell Nature Bob we decided not to cut our potato because we wanted to make the world's tastiest and biggest french fry."

I scratch my head. "I'm not sure if that's a good idea."

"Sure it is," says Carine. And before I have time to stop her, she puts our potato in the pot of oil on the fire.

"Time to fry!" says Nature Bob. He starts

picking up knives and potato slices. "Where's your potato?" he asks when he gets to us.

Carine points to the pot. Nature Bob looks in the pot, and then he looks at us. He has a look on his face like he can't believe what he saw in the pot. "Why didn't you girls cut your potato?" he asks.

"We wanted to make the tastiest *and* biggest french fry," says Carine.

She looks like she's waiting for Nature Bob to say what a good idea that is. But before he can say it, some of the girls start laughing. "You can't fry a whole potato," says a Kool Kat named Chelsea.

"It'll never cook," says another girl.

Taylor shakes her head like just the thought of frying a whole potato is silly. Even Mary Ann is making an *I-don't-see-how-you-could-think-that-cooking-a-whole-potato-is-*

a-good-idea face.

Nature Bob pretends like he's considering the idea, but I can tell he thinks it's a silly idea too. There's more giggling.

I can just imagine what Max is going to say when he hears about this.

I knew when Carine said we should make a big french fry, it sounded totally goofy. I think about what Uncle Al said . . . that it's OK to be goofy.

Then I think about something someone else said. When we woke up this morning, Sandy said today was going to be a big day. But if you ask me, she used the wrong "B" word. She should have said today was going to be a "bad" day, not a "big" day.

BUG BITES

Infirmary, Camp Blue Lake

Dear Mom and Dad,
I'm writing you this letter from the Infirmary, because guess what? I'M IN THE INFIRMARY! You're probably wondering what I'm doing here. It's a very long story, but since I don't have anything else to do except sit here alone on a cot while all of my friends are off doing their activities and having a good

time, I'll tell you.

It all started yesterday morning with Ivy and Nature Bob.

Nature Bob (I don't think Nature is his real first name. I think they just call him Nature Bob because he's really into nature.) and Ivy (that's Nature Bob's assistant, not a plant) are the nature counselors. It's their job to take kids on overnights, and that's where I went last night . . . on an overnight with all the Camp Blue Lake girls.

I was super excited to go on this overnight because you get to go to a special campsite and swim in a pretty lake and cook your food over a fire and tell ghost stories and sleep in a tent.

Except, guess what? For me, it didn't turn out to be so much fun. To tell you the truth, it turned out to be the WORST night of camp for me.

Parts of it were good.

I went to a special campsite. (It sort of looked like our backyard, except that it was a lot bigger and it had a lot more trees and a lake.)

I swam in a pretty lake. (Don't worry, I put on sunscreen before I swam.)

I cooked my food over a fire. (We made hotdogs and French fries and Banana Boats. See recipe at end of letter for more info.)

And I listened to ghost stories. (They were scary, but I remember all of them, and when I come home from camp, I'm going to tell them to Max and try to scare him.)

But one part of it was NOT good at all, and that was the sleeping in a tent part.

The reason it wasn't good was because I had to share a tent with Carine. I wanted to share a tent with Mary Ann (we even brought our matching campfire pajamas), but Nature Bob said we had to share a tent with our bunkmate and here's what happened with mine: Carine brought so much stuff on the overnight that we couldn't fit it all in the tent so we had to leave the tent unzipped a little bit, and when we did, mosquitoes flew inside it while we were sleeping, and they all bit me (I think they should have bitten Carine since it was her fault we had to leave the tent unzipped,

but they didn't bite her, they bit me),
and I had what Nurse Shelby calls an
"allergic reaction," and that's why I'm in
the Infirmary right now instead of out at
my activities having fun.

Now do you see why the overnight
wasn't so much fun for me?

I bet reading this letter and seeing this
picture makes you worried about me. (I
know if I had a 9½-year-old daughter
who looked like that, I'd be worried.)

Well, here's another thing you should
be worried about, and that's my
bunkmate. I feel like camp would be fun
except for one thing. . . . Carine Green.
SHE IS DRIVING ME CRAZY!!!

When I came back to camp after the
overnight, I tried to talk to someone
about it. But no one was very helpful.

Mary Ann and Taylor said that Carine

seems nice and that she didn't mean to leave the tent unzipped.

My counselor said I should give her another chance.

PORTRAIT OF A MOSQUITO'S BEST FRIEND

Nurse Shelby said, "Let's have a look at those bug bites."

Winnie said, "Are you contagious?"

Max said to shake it off (I don't know how you shake off a bug bite) and to put a paper bag over my head so no one would know I'm his sister.

Joey said I'd be better in no time.

I even tried to talk to Uncle Al, who at first said, "Mallory McDonald, is that you under all those bug bites?" Then said he had some words of wisdom for me. He said, "You don't know your friends until you share a tent with them."

Usually, I think Uncle Al's words of wisdom make no sense, but this time, I think he was absolutely right.

That's all for now. G2G. Got to go. G2S. Got to scratch (my bug bites).

Mallory

P.S. Have you considered picking me up early from camp? If you don't know how to get here, just turn left out of

our driveway and drive for a long time until you see a sign that says CAMP BLUE LAKE. I'll be waiting by the gate.

P.P.S. Color War is two days from today, so if you do come to pick me up, please come in two days, and come after dinner so I don't miss Color War, which is supposed to be fun.

P.P.PS. Here's the recipe for Banana Boats (which lucky for me, I got to eat before the mosquitoes ate me) in case you and Dad want to make a campfire in the backyard and try these yourselves.

Banana Boats

Place banana on a piece of foil.
Do NOT remove the peel.
Slice open banana the long way.
Fill banana with mini marshmallows
    and chocolate chips.
Close foil around banana.
Stick it on the fire for 10–15 minutes.
Remove, unwrap, and eat with a spoon.
Say Mmmmm!

Note: If you don't
have a campfire, an
oven will work too.
(But it won't taste
as good because
everything tastes
better when you cook it
over a campfire.)

116

COLOR WAR

**Camp Blue Lake Words of Wisdom:
Color your days bright.**

"Hold still!" says Carine.

I tilt my face up while she puts green glitter shadow on my eyelids. "I'm so glad we're both on the Green Team," she says.

I smile like I'm glad too. But the truth is . . . I'm not so glad. I look around my

bunk. Natalie and Brooke are painting
each other's nails red because they're both
on the Red Team. Nikki and Molly are tying
yellow ribbons onto the ends of each
other's braids.

I think back to last night's dinner. When
Uncle Al read off the teams, I couldn't
believe when I heard Mary Ann and Taylor
were on the Yellow Team, Joey was on the
Blue Team, Max was on the Red Team, and
I was on the Green Team with Carine.

I would have rather been on any other team, even Max's, than on a team with Carine. Ever since we got to camp, I've had to do everything with her.

"Time for Color War to begin!" Sandy says. She holds the bunk door open as we march out and up to the field where the teams are meeting.

When we get to the field, it looks like a four-color rainbow. Everyone is wearing T-shirts in their team colors. Carine and I go to the Green Team meeting place. Our team is already cheering. "Go Green!" everyone screams.

Andie, senior camper and captain of the Green Team, puts her hands on her hips. "If you want to win Color War, you're going to have to yell a whole lot louder!"

Our whole team yells *Go Green* at the top of our lungs. And we're not the only ones

yelling. The Blue and Yellow and Red Teams are all cheering for their team to win.

"Campers, your attention please," Uncle Al shouts through a megaphone. "In just a few minutes, Color War will begin. But before it does, I want to wish all four teams good luck. Today is not only about competition, it's also about team spirit and having fun. Work with your teammates and help each other."

Winnie, who is also on the Green Team, rolls her eyes. "I bet he's about to give us some Words of Wisdom too."

And Winnie is right.

"The Camp Blue Lake Words of Wisdom

for the day . . . *Color your days bright.*"

Winnie shakes her head. "I have no idea what Uncle Al is talking about."

Actually, I don't either, but neither of us has long to think about it because Andie starts asking for volunteers.

"Color War is made up of all sorts of competitions between the four teams," Andie explains. "It's my job as captain to organize our team to compete in all of the activities. Who wants to compete in the swimming race?" she asks.

I raise my hand.

Carine raises her hand. "Mallory and I can do it together," she says. "This will be fun," she says to me after Andie writes our names down.

I can't believe I'm doing something else with Carine. I cross my arms across my chest. I don't say a word while Andie asks for volunteers to go to archery, gymnastics, land sports, guitar, and canoeing. Some of those activities sound like fun, but I know if I raise my hand, Carine will too.

"OK, team," says Andie. "I have a special job. Who wants to go to the Craft Shop and paint the team sign?"

My hand flies up in the air before I can stop it. "I'll do the sign," I say.

"Great," Andie says. "I need one more sign painter."

And faster than I can say *Go Green,* someone else raises a hand, and that someone is Carine.

We do another team cheer, and then

Andie sends everyone off to their activities. Carine and I walk to the waterfront. I don't say anything while we walk. I can't believe Carine signed up for the same activities as I did. I feel like no matter what I do, she does it too.

When we get to the waterfront, Mike, the diving counselor, tells us we're competing in a backstroke race. "Team with the fastest time wins."

Carine and I start to walk down the dock to our station, then Carine stops. "Mallory, it's really hot out here. Did you put on sunscreen?"

I shake my head *no.*

"I'm going to run back to the cabin to get some," says Carine.

I look at the end of the dock where the other teams are lining up. "Hurry! You don't want to miss the race."

"I'll hurry," says Carine. I hope she hurries. I walk to the end of the dock and line up with campers from the other teams.

I look at the beach. No sign of Carine anywhere.

Mike starts counting campers. "We should have two campers from each team," he says. "We're short one."

I explain to him that Carine went to get something and that she'll be right back.

Mike looks at his watch. "We can wait for a minute, but not much longer."

I look at the beach again and up the hill. Still no sign of Carine.

Mike wipes a bead of sweat from his forehead. "We need to get started," says Mike. "If you don't have two swimmers, I'm afraid the Green Team will be disqualified from this event." He looks like he's sorry he has to say that.

I look up the hill for Carine. *Where is she?*

Mike blows his whistle and kids from the Yellow, Blue, and Red Teams take their turns doing the backstroke. The Red Team cheers when Mike announces that they won. "Everyone needs to go to their next activity," Mike tells us.

I walk down the dock towards the Craft Shop. I can't believe Carine didn't get back in time and we were disqualified. As I walk up the hill, I see Taylor and Mary Ann. I run to catch up to them. When I do, I tell them what happened on the dock.

"Ever since I got to camp, I've had to do everything with Carine," I tell Mary Ann and Taylor. "And no matter what we've done, whether it's been keeping our shelves neat, or being waterfront buddies, or trying to make french fries, or going on an overnight, or competing in a backstroke race, she's found a way to mess it up."

"I'm sure she doesn't mean to mess things up," says Mary Ann.

"And she seems nice," says Taylor.

"I know she doesn't mean to mess things up, and she is nice. I'm just sick of doing everything with . . . "

But before I can say who I'm sick of doing everything with, a familiar voice interrupts me.

"Sorry it took so long," says Carine. "I couldn't find the sunscreen."

I look at Carine. She has a funny look on her face, and so do Mary Ann and Taylor.

"Shouldn't you be on the dock?" she asks.

I swallow hard. I hope her funny look is a *why-aren't-you-on-the-dock* look and not an *I-heard-what-you-said-and-I-hope-you-weren't-talking-about-me* look. "We were disqualified," I tell Carine.

Carine's shoulders drop. "Is it because I wasn't there in time?"

I nod my head *yes*. Even though it was her fault, I still feel badly telling her, especially after what just happened.

"I'm sorry," she says. "I . . . "

But I interrupt Carine before she can say anything else. "Let's just make the sign."

"OK," says Carine. When we walk into the Craft Shop, kids from the Blue and Red Teams are already there making signs.

"You girls need paint and paper," says Lara the arts and crafts counselor. She points Mary Ann and me towards the supply closet to get the paint.

Mary Ann takes a plastic tub of yellow paint off the shelf. "There's the green," she says. I take the green tub of paint off the shelf.

When we walk out of the supply closet, Carine is already set up in a corner with paper and sketching pencils. She waves to me. "Mallory, over here."

I toss the tub of green paint in Carine's direction. She reaches up to catch it, but when she does, something happens that I

did NOT think would happen. THE LID
COMES OFF! GREEN PAINT SPILLS ALL OVER
CARINE!

Her shirt and shorts and hair and face
and even her eyelashes are covered in
paint.

CARINE GREEN IS TOTALLY GREEN!

Everyone in the Craft Shop sucks in their
breath.

Carine doesn't make a sound. I've never
seen her so quiet, or so green.

Taylor and Mary Ann and Lara all rush
over to her. "Are you OK?" asks Taylor.

"Are you hurt?" asks Mary Ann.

Lara hands Carine some paper towels.
But Carine doesn't take them. She just
stands there . . . dripping green paint.

"At least you're showing your team
spirit," I say. I try to make a joke, to get
Carine to laugh. But she doesn't laugh, and

neither does anyone else. In fact, no one is laughing. All they're doing is looking, and the thing they are looking at is me.

Lara has a funny look on her face. It's a *why-would-you-throw-someone-a-tub-of-paint-without-making-sure-the-top-was-screwed-on-tight* look on her face.

Taylor and Mary Ann have looks on their faces too. But nothing about their looks is funny. To me, they both have *did-you-do-it-on-purpose?* looks on their faces.

I think about what I told them on our way to the Craft Shop. I was mad at Carine, but I would never throw paint on her on purpose. I hope they don't think I did. I look at Carine, and she has the same look on her face as Taylor and Mary Ann.

"Carine, I'm so sorry. I didn't know the lid wasn't on tight. Are you OK?"

But Carine doesn't look OK. It's like the

paint is glue, and except for the look on her face, none of her parts are moving.

Lara takes a deep breath. "Mallory, please take Carine to the Infirmary."

Carine doesn't look like she wants to go anywhere, especially with me. But I do what Lara says. Everyone is quiet as I take Carine out of the Craft Shop.

I think about Uncle Al's Words of Wisdom this morning. When he said to color your days bright, I don't think this was what he had in mind.

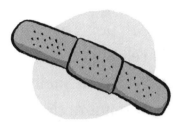

IN THE INFIRMARY

Camp Blue Lake Infirmary
Words of Wisdom:
Some ailments hurt more on the
inside than they do on the outside.

"What happened?!?" Nurse Shelby sucks
in her breath when she sees Carine.

Carine doesn't answer, so I answer for her. "Some green paint accidentally spilled all over her," I tell Nurse Shelby.

"Hmmm," says Nurse Shelby, like she's considering how paint accidentally spills all over someone. "I've seen sore throats, scraped knees, and bug bites, but I've never seen anyone covered in green paint. Are you hurt?" she asks Carine.

Carine shakes her head *no*.

Nurse Shelby taps her foot like she's waiting for an explanation that makes sense. I tell her how the paint spilled on Carine in the Craft Shop.

"I see," she says when I finish. But if you ask me, it doesn't seem like she sees at all. She has the same look on her face that she had when she gave our bunk a Stinko during cabin inspections. "Let's get you into the shower," she says to Carine.

Carine doesn't move.

The only thing I see moving is a tear running down her cheek. A green tear. "It wasn't an accident," Carine says quietly. "Mallory did it on purpose."

"It was an accident!" I tell Carine.

Nurse Shelby looks at me, then she looks

at Carine. "Carine, why would Mallory spill paint on you on purpose?"

Carine crosses her arms across her chest and drops of green paint fall onto the Infirmary floor. She looks at me. "I heard what you said to Mary Ann and Taylor. You said that I mess up everything, and that you're sick of doing things with me."

Carine stops talking. Her lip is trembling.

"It's OK." Nurse Shelby rubs the paint-free part of Carine's back. "I don't think Mallory would say something like that." Then she looks at me. "Mallory, you didn't say that, did you?"

Now I'm the one who is quiet.

"Mallory, did you say that?" asks Nurse Shelby.

I take a deep breath. "I said it, but I only said it because I was mad about Carine going back to the cabin and being disqualified from the backstroke race."

I cross my toes that Carine will understand, but it doesn't look like she does. Fresh green tears roll down her cheeks. "Do you know why I went back to the bunk?"

I nod. "You went back to get sunscreen."

"For you," says Carine. "I went back to get sunscreen for you because it was so sunny and I didn't want your freckles to burn."

Now I feel like I'm going to cry. I think back to the *I-want-you-to-wear-sunscreen-so-your-freckles-don't-burn* conversation I had with Mom before I left for camp. Carine must care about me a lot if she cares about my freckles.

I think about what Mom and Dad said about giving things a chance. I wish I had given Carine a chance to explain why she went back to the bunk instead of saying what I did to Taylor and Mary Ann. "Carine, I'm sorry about what I said. I shouldn't have said it." I hope Carine will accept my apology.

But Carine doesn't look like she wants to accept anything, not even a tissue from Nurse Shelby. She just stands there dripping green paint and crying green tears.

Nurse Shelby takes a deep breath. "You girls have a lot of talking to do later. But right now, Carine needs to take a shower and you need to go back to Color War."

She points Carine towards the bathroom and me towards the door.

I start to leave the Infirmary. Then I stop. I hate leaving without Carine knowing how awful I feel about saying what I did. I turn around to say something, but when I do Nurse Shelby points to the

TALE OF A PAINT SPILLER
CATCH!
BOO-HOO!
BAD PAINT SPILLER
I'M SORRY!

door like it's time for me to leave.

I watch Carine as she walks toward the bathroom. She leaves a little trail of green paint behind her. Even though I know how much Carine loves green, right now I think even she'd say there's such a thing as too much green.

As I walk out of the Infirmary, I read the Camp Blue Lake Words of Wisdom that are on a little plaque on the wall.

Some ailments hurt more on the inside than they do on the outside.

I know it must feel horrible on the outside to be covered in wet paint, but I'm sure Carine feels even worse on the inside thinking that I'm sick of doing things with her and that I think she messes everything up.

I kick a rock along the path as I walk towards the Lodge. Everyone is coming out after lunch. Mary Ann and Taylor run up to me. So do Max, Winnie, and Joey.

"Hey Mallory, how's Carine?" asks Mary Ann.

"I can't believe you spilled paint on her," says Winnie.

"Way to go," says Max. "The whole camp is talking about you."

"Is she OK?" asks Taylor.

My stomach grumbles, but I don't think it's because I missed lunch. I shrug my shoulders. I don't feel like talking to anybody about Carine. I did that once today and now everything's a mess.

"Hey Mallory, I got your mail," says Joey. He hands me a letter. I take it and go sit down by myself on a stump. I don't want to talk to anybody about anything right now. I open my envelope and start reading.

Dear Mallory,

We got your last letter and were very sorry to hear that the overnight didn't go so well. We hope your bug bites cleared up.

By the time you get this letter, you will probably be celebrating Color War.

We know that will be fun. We can't wait to hear what team you were on. (Is there a Purple Team? We hope you were on it since that's your favorite color.)

Write and tell us everything. We want to hear about your activities, your counselor, the girls in your cabin, and particularly about your bunkmate, Carine. Daddy says to tell you he's sure she didn't mean to leave the tent unzipped and that everyone, especially bunkmates, deserves a second chance.

We love you!
Mom and Dad

P.S. Tell Max to write his own letter!

I fold my letter and put it back into the envelope. I think about what Dad said about second chances. I wish I had given Carine one.

I pretend like I'm at the wish pond on my street. I close my eyes and make a wish.

I wish Carine Green will give me a second chance.

A CAMPFIRE

**Camp Blue Lake Words of Wisdom:
Keep the campfires burning.**

A few important facts:

Fact #1: The Green Team won Color War.

Fact #2: I should be really happy since I was on the Green Team.

Fact #3: I'm not happy at all because Carine hasn't spoken to me since Color

War and tonight is the last night of camp
and if we don't speak tonight then we're
going to go home not speaking and that
doesn't seem like a good way to end camp.

The problem is . . . I don't know how to
get Carine to speak to me.

I tried talking to her, but she told Natalie
to tell me that she didn't want to hear
what I had to say. I tried talking to Sandy,
who said she tried talking to Carine, who
said she would not talk to me. Period.

I roll over in my bed and look at my
watch. There's still half an hour of rest
hour left. I climb down off of my bunk and
walk outside to the front of the cabin,
where Sandy is trying to stuff her sleeping
bag into a little plastic bag that looks way
too small to hold a big sleeping bag.
"Sandy, can I talk to you?"

"Is it about Carine?" she asks. "We've

talked about it so many times and I really don't know what else to say."

"I just wanted to know if I could leave the bunk during rest hour."

Sandy stops stuffing. "You know the rule: No one leaves during rest hour."

"Please, it's really important."

"Where do you want to go?" she asks.

"I want to go to the Kool Kats bunk. I know Mary Ann will be able to help me solve my problem with Carine."

Sandy smiles at me. "I think we can make an exception."

I thank Sandy and run down the path to the Kool Kat's bunk. Mary Ann is outside hanging a bathing suit on the clothesline.

"Hey," I say to Mary Ann.

"What are you doing here?" she asks.

"Sandy said it was OK." I sit down on a rock behind Mary Ann's cabin. "Carine still won't talk to me."

Mary Ann sits down beside me. "Still?"

I nod my head *yes.* I told Mary Ann yesterday and the day before about Carine not talking to me, and now it's been three days since we've spoken. "It's the last day of camp and I have to think of some way to tell her how sorry I am."

"Maybe you could give her a key log," says Mary Ann.

I think about the Key Log Ceremony we're having at the Campfire tonight. Uncle Al explained that since tonight is the last night of camp, there's a Camp Blue Lake tradition that if there's something important you want to say to someone, you can say it tonight at the Campfire. Then he said you can put a special little log, called a key log, on the fire for that person.

"I'm definitely going to do that," I tell Mary Ann.

But I'd like to do something else too.

"Carine thinks that I don't want to be her friend. I want to do something special to show her that I'm glad we're friends."

"Like what?" asks Mary Ann.

I shrug my shoulders. "That's the problem. I can't think of anything. Will you help me?"

Mary Ann wraps her arm around me. "Of course I'll help you."

Even though we weren't in the same bunk and didn't spend as much time together at camp as I wanted to, Mary Ann will always be my best friend. "Thanks," I say.

"That's what best, best, best friends are for," says Mary Ann. "But we better think of something fast because rest hour will be over soon."

Mary Ann is right. We have to hurry.

"Maybe you could write her a note or make up a poem for her," says Mary Ann.

I shake my head. "I want to give her something more special than that."

"Hmmm," says Mary Ann like she's thinking.

I'm thinking too. I rub the sides of my head to help me think, and when I do, I get

an idea. "I've got it!" I say to Mary Ann. I
don't know why I didn't think of it before.
Even though there's no one behind the
cabin except the two of us, I lean over and
whisper my plan in Mary Ann's ear.

"It's perfect!" says Mary Ann. "But you
better hurry."

Mary Ann is right. I do have to hurry. I
run back to my bunk. Sandy is still outside.
I tell her what I want to do. Then I cross my
toes. I hope she says *yes.*

"I think Carine will love that," says
Sandy. "Now go!"

I run as fast as I can to the Craft Shop.
When I get there, Lara is inside, wrapping
ceramic bowls in tissue paper. "Did you
come to pick this up?" She hands me the
bowl I made for Cheeseburger.

"I'll take it," I say. "But I came for
another reason." I tell Lara about my plan.

"You can use anything you want, except for green paint." Lara winks at me.

I take what I need from the supply closet. Then I get to work. I work while Lara wraps pots. I work really fast since I don't have much time. When I'm done, I put what I made in my pocket. I thank Lara and I run back to my bunk.

When I get there, everyone is packing and getting ready for tonight's Campfire and writing bus notes to give out for the trip home tomorrow.

"Welcome back, Mallory," Sandy says when she sees me. "Everything OK?"

I nod that it is. Then I give Sandy a hug. "Thanks for letting me go."

Sandy hugs me back. "I like what you're doing, and I think Carine will too."

My last afternoon at camp goes by faster than a good episode of my favorite TV show, *Fashion Fran.* I feel like someone put the camp clock on fast forward.

After dinner, everyone walks to the Campfire Ring.

"I can't believe this is our last night," says Brooke.

"After Campfire, all we have left is Cilk and Mookies," says Molly.

I think about what I'm doing *after* Cilk and Mookies. When I told Mary Ann and Sandy, they both liked my plan. I cross my toes. I hope Carine will too.

Uncle Al walks to the front of the Campfire Ring. He beats softly on a little drum until all of the campers sitting on logs around the fire are quiet.

"It's officially time for the Camp Blue Lake Key Log Ceremony to begin," says Uncle Al. He points to a pile of small logs in front of the fire. "Camp is coming to a close. I'd like everyone to take a moment to think about the special friends you've made this summer."

I watch the sun setting over the lake. I think about Carine. Even though she did lots of things that were annoying, she was a nice friend. I really hope she likes what I have to say.

Uncle Al bends down and picks up a log. "I'd like to invite anyone who'd like to, to come up, put a log on the fire, and say a few words."

A big group of the oldest campers goes up first. They all pick up key logs and start reading messages that they've written for each other. Some of them start crying.

More campers start going up to the campfire. Young campers. Old campers. Even campers from my street. Joey puts a log on the fire for one of his soccer friends. Winnie puts a log on the fire for a girl in her bunk. Even Max goes up to put a log on the fire for the boys on the Camp Blue Lake Baseball Team.

I reach down and take the piece of paper with the message I've written for Carine out of my pocket. I walk to the campfire and pick up a key log. When it's

my turn, I take a deep breath and start.

"This key log is for Carine Green. As bunkmates, we've learned a lot about each other. One of the things I've learned is that good friends deserve a second chance. You've been a great friend to me. I'm sorry about what I said, and I hope you'll give me a second chance."

When I'm done reading, I put my key log on the fire. I walk towards Carine.

"I'm really sorry," I whisper.

She smiles like she accepts my apology. "Mallory, that was so sweet," she says.

I'm glad Carine liked what I said, but I still feel badly about what happened. "Carine, I didn't spill the paint on you on purpose."

"I know," says Carine.

I give Carine a hug, and she hugs me back. When we sit down, Sandy puts an arm around both of us. "Girls, I'm thrilled to see you're working out your differences. That's what camp is all about."

"OK," says Uncle Al after the last camper puts their key log on the fire. "It's time to sing Taps and go back to our bunks. The busses leave bright and early tomorrow morning, so we want you all to try and get a good night's sleep."

A lot of campers start laughing. "Uncle Al knows that no one sleeps the last night of camp," says Natalie.

Uncle Al beats on his drum. "Campers, attention please. Before we leave, I'd like to share with you my final Words of Wisdom for the summer."

"We know what you're going to say," some of the oldest campers shout out.

But Uncle Al says it anyway. "Keep the campfires burning!"

I think about what he said. I think Uncle Al is saying to keep the happy memories of camp burning in your mind like a big, bright campfire. And that's exactly what I'm planning to do. Just thinking about it makes me smile.

Then, I feel someone jiggle my arm. "Earth to Mallory," says Carine. "The campfire is over!" I pop up off the log I'm sitting on.

It's time to put Operation *Last-Night-of-Camp* into action.

FRIENDS FOREVER

**Camp Blue Lake Words of Wisdom:
Saying good-bye is never easy.**

"Carine and I will get the Cilk and
Mookies," I tell Sandy.

Sandy winks at me. We've already
talked about the plan. She knows what I'm

doing. "I'm glad to see the two of you working together again," she says. "But hurry back. It's our last night at camp, and I want all of my Duckies together."

"No problem," I tell Sandy. I grab Carine's hand. "C'mon!" I whisper as we leave the bunk. "We've got a lot to do and not much time to do it."

"All we have to do is get Cilk and Mookies," says Carine.

"Um, not exactly!"

Carine and I run to the Lodge. When we get there, I push the door open. "First stop, Cilk and Mookies!"

I hand Carine the milk carton and cups. "You take the Cilk, and I'll take the Mookies." I grab the big bag labeled *Lucky Ducks* off of the table. "Now we have someplace special to go."

Carine follows me out of the Lodge as I

run towards the Campfire Ring.

"It looks different without the fire and all the people who were here earlier," I say. "But it seemed like the best place."

Carine looks confused. "For what?"

I reach into my pocket and pull out the matching friendship bracelets I made in the Craft Shop this afternoon. "For our Friendship Bracelet Ceremony."

I clear my throat. "Carine Green, it's officially time for our Friendship Ceremony to begin." I hold out both bracelets and shine the flashlight so Carine can see them.

"They're purple and green!" says Carine. Then she looks at me like she likes the combination. "Green is my favorite color, and purple is your favorite color."

I tie a bracelet on Carine's wrist and she ties one on mine.

"OK," I say when we're done. "Hook your

pinky around mine and repeat after me:
I do solemnly swear to never take off this
friendship bracelet until next summer."

Carine repeats what I said. Then she
says something of her own. "Mallory,
thanks for making the bracelets. That was
really sweet of you." She looks down at her

wrist. "Now I have two favorite colors."

I look down at our bracelets. "I just wanted you to know that I'm really glad we're friends," I say to Carine.

Carine smiles. "Me too." Then she stops smiling. "I'll tell you who won't be glad if we don't get back to the bunk soon with the Cilk and Mookies."

"The Lucky Ducks!" we say together. She grabs the Cilk and I grab the Mookies and we run down the path.

"What took you two so long?" Brooke asks when we get back to the bunk.

"We were just getting Cilk and Mookies," Carine says innocently.

Sandy winks at Carine and me, then we all sit down on her bed while she passes around Cilk and Mookies.

"I can't believe tonight is our last night," says Nikki.

"I'm so sad we have to leave tomorrow," says Natalie.

Sandy puts one arm around Nikki and the other around Natalie. "You know what Uncle Al says about that."

Nikki smiles. "Saying good-bye is never easy."

"That's right," says Sandy. "But at least we have the great Camp Blue Lake tradition of bus notes."

When we finish our Cilk and Mookies, everyone passes around the bus notes that we made for each other.

When I have all of mine, I take my backpack out from under my bed and slip them carefully inside so I can read them on the bus on the way home tomorrow.

I think back to the day I got on the bus to come here. I didn't want to come to camp, and now I don't want to leave. "Hey

Sandy, can we stay up late tonight?" I ask.

"On one condition." Sandy has a serious look on her face. "You all promise to come back next year."

"We promise," we all say together.

I look around my cabin at all of the good friends I've made. Even though parts of camp were hard, I think about all of the fun I've had and the friends I've made. Mom and Dad were right about giving camp, and people, a chance. I'm really glad I did.

Then I think about Uncle Al's Words of Wisdom. Saying good-bye is never easy. But promising to come back next summer is a breeze.

Last night, Camp Blue Lake
(writing this by flashlight in my bed)

Dear Mom and Dad,
    This is a quickie because you'll see me
tomorrow. (Actually you'll see me before
you see this letter.) This is the last night
of camp and I just have one question: Did
you sign me up to come back to camp
next year?
    I hope so. It is A.V.I.T.T.D.! That is short
for A Very Important Thing to Do.
    Thanks and see you soon, soon, soon!

Big huge hugs and kisses,
Mallory

P.S. No P.S's. It's the last night of
camp, and I want to spend every minute
with my bunkmates!

BUS NOTES

I can't believe it was just two weeks ago that I was on this very same bus going *to* camp, and now I'm coming home *from* camp.

I'm so, so, so sad camp is over!

Even though I wasn't sure I wanted to go, one thing I'm completely sure about is that I don't want to leave.

I already miss all of my new friends, but at least I have the bus notes they gave me to keep me company.

Here are a few of the ones I like the best:

Hey Mallory!

How is your bus ride so far? I can't believe camp is over. Boo Hoo! I already miss you so much. I know being bunkmates didn't start out great, but it ended fantastic! I hope we get to be bunkmates again next summer. You are such a great friend. Hopefully, we'll be able to see each other sometime during the year!

Miss and luv u lots!

Carine Green
(not my hair color, just my name)

P.S. I love my friendship bracelet!

Hi Mal Gal,

Wasn't camp like so, so, so cool? I hope you don't mind that I love saying things three times. Camp was the best, best, best and so are you! Don't forget to wear your Camp Blue Lake T-shirt a lot this winter. I'm never going to take mine off!

Taylor

Dear Camper Mallory,

I sure am going to miss you! I feel so lucky that you were one of my Ducks! I'm so glad I got to be your counselor. Have a great school year. I can't wait to see you next summer on the shores of Blue Lake.

Love,
Sandy

Mallory,

I'm not going to write much because I know you'll be sitting in the bus seat next to me when you read this. I'm right, aren't I? I know some things changed this summer. We both made new friends. But here is one thing that will never change: you will always be my best, best, best friend at home or camp or anywhere else.

Hugs, Hugs, Hugs!
Kisses, Kisses, Kisses!
Mary Ann

P.S. I can't believe when we get off this bus, we will be next door neighbors again. Wow! Wow! Wow! I can't wait.

CAMP PICS

I counted the days until camp starts next summer. Exactly 339 days until I get to go back to Camp Blue Lake. I don't know how I'm going to be able to wait that long! I made a special scrapbook of my favorite camp pics so I can look at them every day.

This is me with my bunk. I'm going to miss the Lucky Ducks soooooo much!

This is me with Carine. She turned out to be the W.B.B. That's short for World's Best Bunkmate.

And this is me back home in Fern Falls with Max and Joey and Winnie and Mary Ann. Even though camp is over, I still feel like a lucky duck because some of my best camp friends are also my best home friends.

I know what you're thinking . . . that you'd never hear me, Mallory McDonald, say I feel like a lucky duck, but I do. Going to sleep-away camp was a lot like moving and going to a new school. I had no idea what it would be like, but once I gave it a chance, it turned out to be a lot better than I ever expected.

I'm so, so, so glad I went to camp!

Darby Creek
A division of Lerner Publishing Group, Inc.
241 First Avenue North
Minneapolis, MN 55401 USA

For reading levels and more information,
look up this title at www.lernerbooks.com.

Library of Congress Cataloging-in-Publication Data

Friedman, Laurie B.
    Campfire Mallory / by Laurie Friedman ; illustrations by Jennifer Kalis.
        p.   cm.
    Summary: Nine-and-a-half-year-old Mallory's trepidation about going to sleep-away camp is multiplied when she and her best friend are assigned to different cabins, and a new "friend" seems determined to get Mallory in trouble.
    ISBN: 978-0-8225-7657-0 (lib. bdg. : alk. paper)
    ISBN: 978-0-7613-4019-5 (EB pdf)
    [1. Camps—Fiction. 2. Best friends—Fiction. 3. Friendship—Fiction. 4. Conduct of life—Fiction.] I. Kalis, Jennifer, ill. II. Title.
    PZ7.F89773Cam 2008
    [Fic]—dc22   2007022218

Manufactured in the United States of America
15 - 52183 - 8586 - 11/22/2021